FOREX TRADING FOR BEGINNERS

TABLE OF CONTENT

INTRODUCTION

The FX market has existed for millennia, at least in its most fundamental form. To buy products and services, people have long exchanged or bartered items and money. The FX market, as we know it today, is, nonetheless, a very recent invention.

A greater number of currencies were permitted to float freely against one another once the Bretton Woods agreement started to fall apart in 1971. Foreign exchange trading services keep track of individual currency

values, which change depending on supply and demand as well as currency circulation.

Investment and commercial banks carry out

Most trading in the forex markets is done on behalf of clients, however there are other opportunities for speculative trading.

For both experienced investors and amateur ones, compare one currency to another.

When seen as an asset class, currencies have two unique characteristics:

You can generate interest.

between two currencies, a difference.

Changes in the currency rate can benefit you.

Investors may gain from the

by purchasing the currency with the higher interest rate and shorting the currency with the lower interest rate, you can trade the

difference between two interest rates in two distinct economics

Because of the wide interest rate spread during the financial crisis, it was highly usual to short the Japanese yen (JPY) and buy British pounds (GBP). A "carry trade" is another name for this

tactic.

CHAPTER ONE

GETTING STARTED WITH FOREX TRADING

The place where currencies are traded is the FX market. It is the only market in the world that is truly non-stop and continuous. In the past, institutional businesses and sizable banks that represented clients dominated the currency market. But in recent years, it has shifted toward the retail sector, and traders and investors with a range of holding sizes have started to participate.

The absence of physical structures that serve as the markets' trading venues is an intriguing feature of the global currency markets. Instead, it consists of a network of connections created by trading platforms and computer systems. Institutions, investment banks, commercial banks, and retail investors all participate in this market.

Compared to other financial markets, the foreign currency market is thought to be more opaque. In OTC markets, where disclosures are not required, currencies are exchanged. Large institutional corporate liquidity pools are a common aspect of the market. One would assume that the most crucial factor in determining a country's price should be its economic factors. That's not the case, though. 2019 research revealed that the motivations of major financial played the most important role in determining currency prices.

The most significant entities in determining currency exchange rates were:

Three markets—spot markets, forward markets, and futures markets—are the main venues for trading forex. Due to the fact that the spot market serves as the "underlying" asset for the forwards and futures markets, it is the largest of the three markets. The spot market is typically meant when someone mentions the foreign exchange market. Companies and financial institutions who need to hedging their foreign exchange risks out to a certain date in the future tend to use the forwards and futures markets.

Place Market

Because it deals in the largest underlying real asset for the forwards and futures markets, spot market forex trading has historically been the largest. In the past, volumes in forward and futures markets were greater than those in spot markets. However, with the introduction of electronic trading and the growth of forex brokers, the trading volumes for forex spot markets increased.

According to their trading price, currencies are purchased and sold on the spot market. That price is computed based on a number of variables, such as current interest rates, economic performance, and attitudes toward continuing political circumstances (both locally and internationally), and is determined by supply and demand.

perspective of how one currency will perform in the future in comparison to another.

A "spot transaction" is a completed agreement. It is a bilateral transaction in which one party gives the other a certain amount of one currency at the agreed-upon exchange rate in exchange for a specified amount of the other currency. The payment is made in cash when a position has been concluded. Despite the fact that the spot market is sometimes thought of as one that deals with present-day (as opposed to future-day) transactions, the settlement time for these trades is really two days.

Futures and forward markets

A forward contract is a confidential agreement between two parties to purchase a currency on the OTC markets at a future time and at a preset A futures contract is a typical contract between two parties wherein they agree to accept delivery of a currency at a later time and at a predetermined price. Futures are not traded OTC but rather on exchanges. In the forward market, contracts are traded over the counter (OTC) between two parties who agree on the parameters of the deal. On public commodity markets like the Chicago Mercantile Exchange, futures contracts are purchased and sold based on a standard size and settlement date (CME).price.

The National Futures Association (NFA) in the US governs the futures market. Futures contracts include certain requirements, such as the quantity of units being traded, delivery and settlement dates, and non-customizable minimum price increments. When providing clearance and settlement services to the trader, the exchange serves as a counterparty.

Both forms of contracts are legally binding and, though they can be bought and sold prior to expiration, are normally settled for cash at the relevant exchange. When trading currencies, risk can be reduced by using the

forward and futures markets for currencies. Large international firms typically use these markets to protect themselves from potential exchange rate swings, but speculators occasionally participate as well also in these markets.

On several currency pairs, options contracts are traded in addition to forwards and futures. Before the option expires, holders of forex options have the choice, but not the obligation, to engage in a foreign currency transaction at a future date and at a predetermined exchange rate.The forwards, futures, and options markets do not exchange actual currencies, in contrast to the spot market. As an alternative, they work using contracts that indicate claims to a particular currency type, a particular price per unit, and a future date for payment. They are referred to as derivatives markets for this reason.

CHAPTER TWO

WHAT DO WE TRADE IN FOREIGN EXCHANGE MARKET

When businesses transact business outside of their home markets, they run the risk of losing money owing to volatility in currency values. By establishing a rate at which the transaction will be executed, foreign exchange markets offer a mechanism to mitigate currency risk.

To achieve this, a trader can lock in an exchange rate by purchasing or selling currencies in advance on the forward or swap markets. Imagine, for instance, that a business intends to market American-made blenders in Europe at a parity exchange rate between the euro and the dollar (EUR/USD).

The U.S. company hopes to sell the blender for $150, which is competitive with other blenders The blender costs $100 to manufacture, and the U.S. firm plans to sell it for €150, which is competitive with other blenders that were made in Europe. If this plan is successful, then the company will make $50 in profit per sale because the EUR/USD exchange rate is even. Unfortunately, the U.S. dollar began to rise in value vs. the euro until the EUR/USD exchange rate was 0.80, which means it now costs $0.80 to buy €1.00.

The problem facing the company is that while it still costs $100 to make the blender, it can only sell the product at a competitive price of €150—which, when translated back into dollars, is only $120 (€150 x 0.80 = $120). A stronger dollar resulted in a much smaller profit than

expected.

in Europe and costs $100 to produce. The corporation will generate $50 in profit on each sale if this strategy is successful due to the even

EUR/USD exchange rate. Sadly, the U.S. dollar started to appreciate against the euro until the EUR/USD exchange rate reached 0.80, meaning that it now costs $0.80 to buy one euro.

The company's issue is that, even if it still costs $100 to produce the blender, it can only sell it for €150, which, when converted back into dollars, is just $120 (€150 x 0.80 = $120). A stronger dollar led to a significantly lower

By shorting the euro and acquiring the dollar at parity, the blender company may have reduced this risk. In this manner, if the value of the U.S. dollar increased, the gains from trade would make up for the decreased profit from the sale of blenders. If the value of the U.S. dollar declined, the better exchange rate would boost sales revenue for blenders, offsetting any losses in the transaction.

Such hedging is possible in the currency futures market. The fact that futures contracts are standardized and cleared by a centralized body is advantageous to the trader. However, the forwards markets, which are decentralized and part of the interbank system, may be more liquid than currency futures.

Speculators' guide to forex

The supply and demand for currencies are influenced by a number of variables, including interest rates, trade flows, tourism, economic strength, and geopolitical risk, which leads to daily volatility in the foreign exchange markets. Profiting from shifts that could elevate or depreciate the value of one currency in relation to another is possible. Because currencies are traded in pairs, predicting that one currency would weaken is practically the same as predicting that the other currency in the pair will strengthen.

Consider a trader who anticipates higher interest rates in the US than in Australia at a time when the AUD/USD exchange rate is 0.71 (i.e., $0.71 USD is required to purchase $1.00 AUD). According to the dealer, increased U.S. interest rates .

The trader thinks that rising U.S. interest rates will boost demand for dollars, which will lead to a decline in the AUD/USD exchange rate because it will take fewer, stronger dollars to purchase a AUD.

In the event that the trader is right and interest rates increase, the AUD/USD exchange rate will drop to 0.50. In other words, buying $1.00 AUD costs $0.50 USD. The investor would have made money from the value move if they had shorted the AUD and gone long on the USD.

CHAPTER THREE

FOREST TRADE USING TECHNICAL ANALYSIS

Currency traders utilize both technical analysis and fundamental analysis to help them decide when to join and exit the forex market. The most popular type of analysis is by far technical analysis. Principal Analysis

Try valuing an entire nation instead if you believe it's challenging to value one company. The fundamental analysis process is quite intricate in the FX market. It is frequently only used to forecast long-term trends. Some traders do, however, just trade short-term based on news releases. Different times are designated for the release of fundamental indicators of currency values. These consist of:

Farm Workers [3] the Purchasing Managers' Index (PMI)! Consumer Price Index (CPI) [4] [5] Retail Sales!

Durable goods number six! There are other economic reports to pay attention to in addition

to these. Market movements can also result from press releases and news coverage of important government agency meetings. For instance, market volatility may result from remarks made by the head of the Federal Reserve on interest rates. The topics of monetary policy, interest rates, and inflation expectations are discussed at these frequent gatherings.

Therefore, it's crucial for forex traders to be aware of the numerous economic reports to Congress, such as the Humphrey-Hawkins Report and those issued by the Federal Open Market Committee (FOMC).

Fundamental analysts of forex can better comprehend long-term market trends by reading the reports and analyzing the remarks. Short-term traders may discover ways to make money off extraordinary occurrences.

If you decide to do fundamental analysis, be sure to always have a handy economic calendar so you can keep track of when these reports are published. You might also get real-time access to the publication of economic data through your trading platform or broker.

Technical Assessment

Like their colleagues in the equity markets, technical analysts for forex markets examine price movements. The period is the primary distinction between technical analysis in forex and equities. The FX markets are accessible around-the-clock.

As a result, several time-based technical analysis tools need to be adjusted for a 24-hour period. The most popular types of technical analysis in forex are listed below:

Technical indicators include things like Elliott Waves, Fibonacci Studies, Parabolic SAR, and Pivot Points.

A lot of technical analysts combine these research to get more precise forecasts (e.g., the common practice of combining Fibonacci studies with Elliott Waves). Others develop trading

strategies to continually find comparable buying and selling conditions.

CHAPTER FOUR

TRADING TACTICS

A Forex Trading Strategy's Foundations Forex trading strategies can generate trade signals manually or automatically. With manual systems, a trader watches a computer screen for trading signals, interprets them, and then decides whether to buy or sell. Automated systems entail a trader creating an algorithm that identifies trading signals and automatically places transactions. The latter methods eliminate human emotions and may enhance performance.

How to Develop a Forex Trading Strategy Many forex traders begin with a straightforward trading plan. They might see, for instance, that a particular currency pair tends to recover from a certain support or resistance level. They might then elect to include more components that gradually increase the precision of these trading signals. They can demand, for instance, that the price rise from a certain support level by a certain percentage or quantity of pip.

An efficient forex trading strategy is made up of numerous key elements:

Market selection: Traders must decide which currency pairs to trade and develop their ability to read those currency pairs.

2. Position sizing: To manage the level of risk involved in each trade, traders must decide the size of each position.

3. Entry points: Traders need to establish guidelines for when to start a long or short position in a particular currency pair.

4. Exit points: Traders need to create rules that specify when to get out of a winning or losing position, as well as when to exit a long or short position.

5. Trading strategies: Using the appropriate execution technologies is just one of the rules that traders should follow when buying and selling currency pairs.

Trading systems should be created in platforms like MetaTrader, which make automating rule-following simple. These tools also enable users to backtest trading methods to see how well they would have done in the past.

When Should You Change Your Approach?

When traders adhere to the regulations, a forex trading strategy performs quite effectively. What works now might not always work tomorrow since, like anything else, a single method may not always be a one-size-fits-all approach. Before revising a game plan if a strategy isn't working and isn't delivering the expected results, traders may take into account the following:

1. Aligning risk management with trading approach: It could be time to switch tactics if the risk-to-reward ratio is unsuitable.

2. The market environment changes: Depending on certain market trends, a trading strategy may vary if those trends shift.

obsolete. That can indicate that adjustments or changes are necessary.

3. Understanding: A trader's success with a strategy is likely to depend on how well they comprehend it. The usefulness of the approach is lost if a problem arises if a trader is unaware of the restrictions.

A forex trading strategy should not be changed too frequently, even though change might be beneficial. You risk losing if you change your plan of action too frequently.

An Example of a Basic Forex Trading Strategy

Most successful forex traders develop a strategy and perfect it over time. Some focus on one particular study or calculation, while others use broadspectrum analysis to determine their trades. One simple strategy is based on relative interest rate changes between two different countries.

Imagine a trader who expects interest rates to rise in the U.S. compared to Australia while,

The exchange rate is 0.71, meaning that it costs $0.71 USD to buy $1.00 AUD. The trader thinks that when demand for USD increases as a result of higher U.S. interest rates, the AUD/USD exchange rate would decline since it will take fewer, stronger USD to purchase a AUD.

In the event that the trader is right and interest rates increase, the AUD/USD exchange rate will drop to 0.50. In other words, buying $1.00 AUD costs $0.50 USD. The investor would have made money from the value move if they had shorted the AUD and gone long on the USD.

CHAPTER FIVE

HOW TO FIND TRADEBLE STOCKS

There are thousands of stocks available, and day traders can select almost any stock they desire. Therefore, choosing what to trade is the first step for a day trader. Finding ways to profit from a trading opportunity (one stock, several stocks, exchange-traded funds, etc.) follows the identification of the opportunity.

How to Choose Stocks for Liquid Intraday Trading

Stocks that are liquid typically have high volume figures. This makes it possible to buy and sell goods in greater quantities without having a substantial effect on the price. A high level of volume facilitates entry and exit of transactions because intraday trading strategies depend on speed and exact timing. Depth is important because it reveals how much liquidity a stock has at different price points above or below the going bid and ask on the market.

Low to high levels of volatility are seen. In order to profit, day traders need price movement. Stocks that frequently change in value or percentage can be chosen by day traders. Results from these two filters will frequently vary. Large intraday swings are consistently present in stocks that often move 3 percent or more per day. For stocks that often move more than $1.50 every day, the same is true.

Group Members

Most traders seek for stocks that move in conjunction with their industry and index group when making contrarian plays. This implies that when the index or the sector advances, so does the price of the particular stock. If the trader wishes to trade the strongest or weakest stocks every day, then this is crucial. It is good to concentrate on that one stock if a trader chooses to trade the same stock every day;

there is no need to worry about whether it is associated with anything else.

Most traders will find it advantageous to look at companies or ETFs that have at least a moderate to high correlation with the S&P 500 or NASDAQ indexes when choosing the best stocks for intraday trading. Then, pick out the stocks that are comparatively strong or weak in comparison to the index. This is a trading opportunity for day traders because a strong stock may increase by 2% when the index does so by 1%. The stock that moves more offers more potential. Investors should buy equities that are rising faster than the futures when the indices and market futures are heading higher. A robust stock won't decline when the futures do.

Pull back excessively (or may not even pull back at all). These are the stocks to trade during an uptrend as they frequently drive the market higher and, consequently, provide greater potential for profit.

Short selling equities that decline more than the market can be profitable when indexes and market futures are declining. A weak stock won't rise as much when the futures are rising when the market is in a downturn (or will not move up at all). When the market is sliding, weaker stocks have a higher chance of making money.

Although certain sectors may be comparatively strong or weak for weeks at a time, the stocks and ETFs that are stronger or weaker than the market may change daily.

The SPDR S&P 500 and the SPDR Select Technology Fund are compared in the graph below (XLK). In comparison to SPY, the blue line, or XLK, was relatively robust. Both ETFs advanced throughout the day, but XLK was the market leader and beat SPY on a relative basis due to its huge gains on rallies and slightly lower declines on pullbacks. When making a purchase, go for the investment that has the best track record.

For short transactions, the same holds true. Stocks or ETFs that are relatively weak should be avoided by short sellers. This increases the potential profit of the transaction because you are more likely to be in stocks or ETFs that will decline the most when prices do.

Wait with patience for the Pullback Trendlines are merely a rough visual indicator of the start and end points of price waves. As a result, while choosing stocks for intraday trading, you can utilize a trendline to enter the market before the next price wave in the trend's direction.

Similar would be short selling during a downward trend. Wait until the price reaches the trendline with a downward slope. Then, you utilize this as a trading signal to place your entry when the stock starts to go back down.

These two long trades offer a low-risk entrance if you are patient. A few cents below the trendline or the most recent price low made immediately before the entry, the stop-loss level would be where the purchase would be made if it were to fail. There will be lost transactions because trends don't last forever, as was previously stated. But even with the losses, what important is that a profit was generated overall.

Take Consistent Profits

Day traders must invest as little time as possible in deals that are losing money or trending the wrong way because they have a limited amount of time to grab rewards.

Here are two straightforward rules that can be applied to earn from trend trading.

e) When the price is rising or you are holding a long position, you should take profits at or just above the previous price high.

Take gains during a decline or when holding a short position at or just below the preceding trend's low price.

Separating the present market trend from the surrounding noise is a necessary step in choosing the appropriate stocks for intraday trading. So a trader's job is to profit from that trend. The most successful intraday trading equities share a few characteristics, including liquidity, volatility, and correlation. However, it's also crucial to use the appropriate entry and departure strategies.

In this quest, studying trendlines and charting price waves can be helpful. There are numerous trading strategies, but none of them are always successful. Save your money if the setting isn't conducive to implementing your methods.

in case they are.

CHAPTER SIX

HOW TO TRADE SUCCESSFULLY, STEP BY STEP

The finest traders work and maintain discipline to enhance their talents. Additionally, they examine themselves to see what motivates their trading and discover strategies for avoiding the influence of fear and greed. Any forex trader should develop these skills.

Setting Objectives and Trading Style

It is essential to have a concept of your objective and your route before beginning any travel. Therefore, it is crucial to have specific goals in mind and then confirm that your trading strategy can help you achieve these goals. Each trading style has a unique risk profile, thus trading successfully necessitates a particular mindset and strategy.

For instance, you might think about day trading if you have trouble falling asleep while holding a position in the market. On the other side, you might be more of a position trader if you have money that you believe will increase in value over the course of a few months.

The Trading Platform and Broker

Selecting a trustworthy broker is crucial, and learning about the variations among brokers will be quite beneficial. You must be familiar with each broker's procedures and trading policies. Trading in the spot market or over-the-counter market, for instance, differs from trading in exchange-driven marketplaces.

Ensure that the trading platform offered by your broker is appropriate for the analysis you intend to conduct. If you like to trade using Fibonacci numbers, for instance, be sure the broker's

Fibonacci lines can be drawn on a platform. It can be problematic to have a good broker on a decent platform or vice versa.

A Reliable Methodology

As a trader, you should be aware of your decision-making process before entering any market. You must be aware of the data you will require in order to decide whether to enter or leave a transaction. Some traders decide to keep an eye on the fundamentals and charts that underlie the economy to decide when to place the trade. Some people exclusively employ technical analysis. Whatever methodology you select, make sure it is adaptive and consistent. Your system should be able to adapt to the market's shifting dynamics.

Identify Entry and Exit Points Conflicting information that appears when examining charts in various periods causes a lot of traders to become perplexed. On a weekly chart, what appears as a buying opportunity could also be a sell signal on an intraday chart.

Therefore, take sure to synchronize the two if you are getting your fundamental trading direction from a weekly chart and using a daily chart to timing entry. To put it another way, wait until the daily chart also confirms a buy signal if the weekly chart is giving you a recommendation to purchase. Maintain synchronized time.

Establish Your Expectations The formula you use to assess your system's dependability is expectation. Consider all of your previous trades, both winners and losers, and compare them to see how profitable your winning trades were compared to how much money you lost on your losing trades.

Look at your ten most recent trades. Go back to your chart and find the areas where your method would have suggested you should enter and exit trades if you haven't yet placed any actual deals. Determine if you would have made money or lost money. Note down these outcomes.

Even if your trading strategy is effective, there is no assurance that you will make that much money every day you trade because market conditions might change. Here is an illustration of how to calculate expectancy, though:

Expectancy formula expectancy is calculated as follows: (percent Won * Average Win) - (percent Lost * Average Loss).

Illustration of Expectancy

Your win ratio would be 6/10, or 60%, if you made ten trades, six of which were profitable and four of which were unsuccessful.

CHAPTER SEVEN

RISK AND PITFALLS

With an average daily trading volume of more than $5 trillion, the foreign exchange market is the biggest financial market in the world. Despite the fact that there are many forex investors, very few are actually profitable. For the same reasons why investors in other asset classes struggle, many traders also struggle. Additionally, the market's high level of leverage (the use of borrowed money to raise an investment's potential return) and the comparatively low margin requirements for currency trading prevent traders from making a lot of low-risk errors.

Some traders may expect higher investment returns than the market can reliably provide or take on more risk than they would when trading in other markets due to factors unique to currency trading.

The Forex Market, Risks of Trading, Several errors can prevent traders from reaching their financial objectives. The following are some typical hazards that might befall forex traders:

Lack of Trading Discipline: Letting emotions dictate trading decisions is the biggest error any trader can make. A successful forex trader will experience numerous little loses as well as a few large profits. Multiple losses in a row can be emotionally taxing and try a trader's endurance and self-assurance. Cutting wins short and allowing losing trades to spiral out of control might result from trying to beat the market or giving in to fear and greed. Trading within the confines of a well-crafted trading plan that supports sustaining trading discipline enables one to control emotion.

Trading Without a Plan: Making and sticking to a trading plan is the first step to success, whether one trades forex or any other asset class.

Any sort of trading is subject to the saying, "Failing to plan is planning to fail." Successful traders use a written strategy that incorporates risk management guidelines and details the anticipated return on investment (ROI). Investors can avoid some of the most common trading hazards by adhering to a strategic trading plan; if you don't have a plan, you're underestimating your potential in the forex market.

Failing to Adjust to the Market: You should make a plan for each trade before the market even begins. Large, unforeseen losses can be greatly decreased by performing scenario analysis and planning the actions and countermoves for every possible market situation. There are new opportunities and threats as the market evolves. No magic bullet or flawless "method" can consistently win out over time. The best traders adjust to market fluctuations and tweak their techniques to fit them. Planning for low likelihood events helps successful traders avoid being caught off guard when they do occur. They keep ahead of the competition and continually come up with fresh,

original ways to profit from the changing market through a process of education and adaptation.

Learning Through Trial and Error: Without a doubt, trial and error is the most expensive method of learning to trade the currency markets. It is not an effective technique to trade any market to figure out the right trading tactics through trial and error. Since the forex market differs greatly from the equities market, it is likely that rookie traders will suffer losses that will have a devastating effect on their accounts. Accessing the knowledge of successful traders is the most effective technique to become a successful forex trader. This can be accomplished through formal trade instruction or by working with a mentor who has a distinguished background. Shadowing a good trader is one of the best methods to hone your skills, especially after putting in hours of practice.

Having unrealistic expectations: Contrary to what some people may believe, forex trading is

not a quick-money program. It takes a long time to become good enough to earn money; it's not a sprint. The tactics involved must be mastered repeatedly for success. Trading with more capital at risk than the potential rewards is frequently the result of swinging for the fences or trying to drive the market to deliver extraordinary returns. Giving up risk and money management guidelines that are intended to minimize market remorse means giving up trade discipline in order to gamble on irrational gains.

Poor Money and Risk Management: When developing a strategy, traders should focus just as much on risk management.

Some gullible people may trade without protection and avoid employing stop losses and similar strategies because of concern that they will be stopped out too early. Successful traders are always aware of the exact amount of their investment capital that is at risk and are confident that it is reasonable given the anticipated rewards. Capital preservation

becomes more crucial as the trading account gets bigger.

Combining the right position sizing with a variety of trading methods and currency pairs can protect a trading account from irrecoverable losses.

Controlling Leverage

Despite the fact that these errors can happen to all different kinds of investors and traders, problems with the currency market can greatly raise trading risks. Because of the substantial financial leverage available to forex traders, there are additional dangers that need to be controlled.

Using leverage gives traders the chance to increase returns. Leverage and the associated financial risk, however, are a double-edged

sword that magnifies both the potential loss and upside. The ability to leverage an account up to 400:1 in the forex market enables traders to achieve both large trading profits and crippling trading losses. Although the market permits traders to take on enormous amounts of risk, it is frequently in their best interests to keep their usage of leverage to a minimum.

The majority of experienced traders leverage their accounts by roughly 2:1, trading one normal lot ($100,000) for every $50,000 they have available. This equates to one micro lot ($1,000) for every $500 of the account value and one mini lot ($10,000) for every $5,000. The amount of margin that brokers demand for each trade determines the degree of

leverage that is available. Simply put, a margin call is a good faith deposit you make to protect your broker from possible transaction losses. In order to conduct transactions with the interbank market, the bank pools all of the margin deposits into a single, very sizable margin deposit. The terrifying margin call, in which brokers demand more cash deposits, is well known to everyone who has ever had a trade go tragically wrong;

Because their capitalization levels fall short of the size of the trades they execute, many forex traders lose money. Forex traders are forced to take on such a significant and fragile financial risk either because of greed or the possibility of controlling enormous sums of money with only a little quantity of capital.

For instance, with a leverage ratio of 100:1 (a fairly typical leverage ratio), it only takes a 1% change in price to cause a 100% loss. Additionally, each loss—even the minor ones brought on by being forced to exit a trade too soon—only makes the situation worse by decreasing the overall account balance and raising the leverage ratio.

Leverage not only makes losses bigger, but it also raises transaction expenses as a percentage of account value. For instance, if a trader with a $500 mini account buys five mini lots ($10,000) of a currency pair with a five-pip spread using 100:1 leverage, the trader will additionally pay $25 in transaction fees (1/pip x 5 pip spread) x 5 lots. They have to catch up before the trade ever takes place because the

$25 in transaction expenses equals 5% of the account value. Transaction costs rise as a percentage of account value with increasing leverage, and they also rise as account value declines.

Many of the same problems that trouble investors in other asset classes also hamper FX traders. Building a relationship with other experienced forex traders who can impart to you the trading disciplines required by the asset class, including the risk and money management rules required to trade the forex market, is the simplest method to avoid some of these errors.

www.ingramcontent.com/pod-product-compliance
Lightning Source LLC
LaVergne TN
LVHW052105160826
845678LV00015B/3366